The Tool Box Book

by Ellen Weiss

Illustrated by Richard Brown

A SESAME STREET/GOLDEN PRESS BOOK
Published by Western Publishing Company, Inc.
in conjunction with Children's Television Workshop.

Library of Congress Catalog Card Number: 80-67282
ISBN 0-307-23121-6

*Featuring
Jim Henson's
Sesame Street
Muppets*

Mr. Hooper is getting out the toolbox
because today is Do-It Day on Sesame Street.
In the toolbox there is a tool for every job.

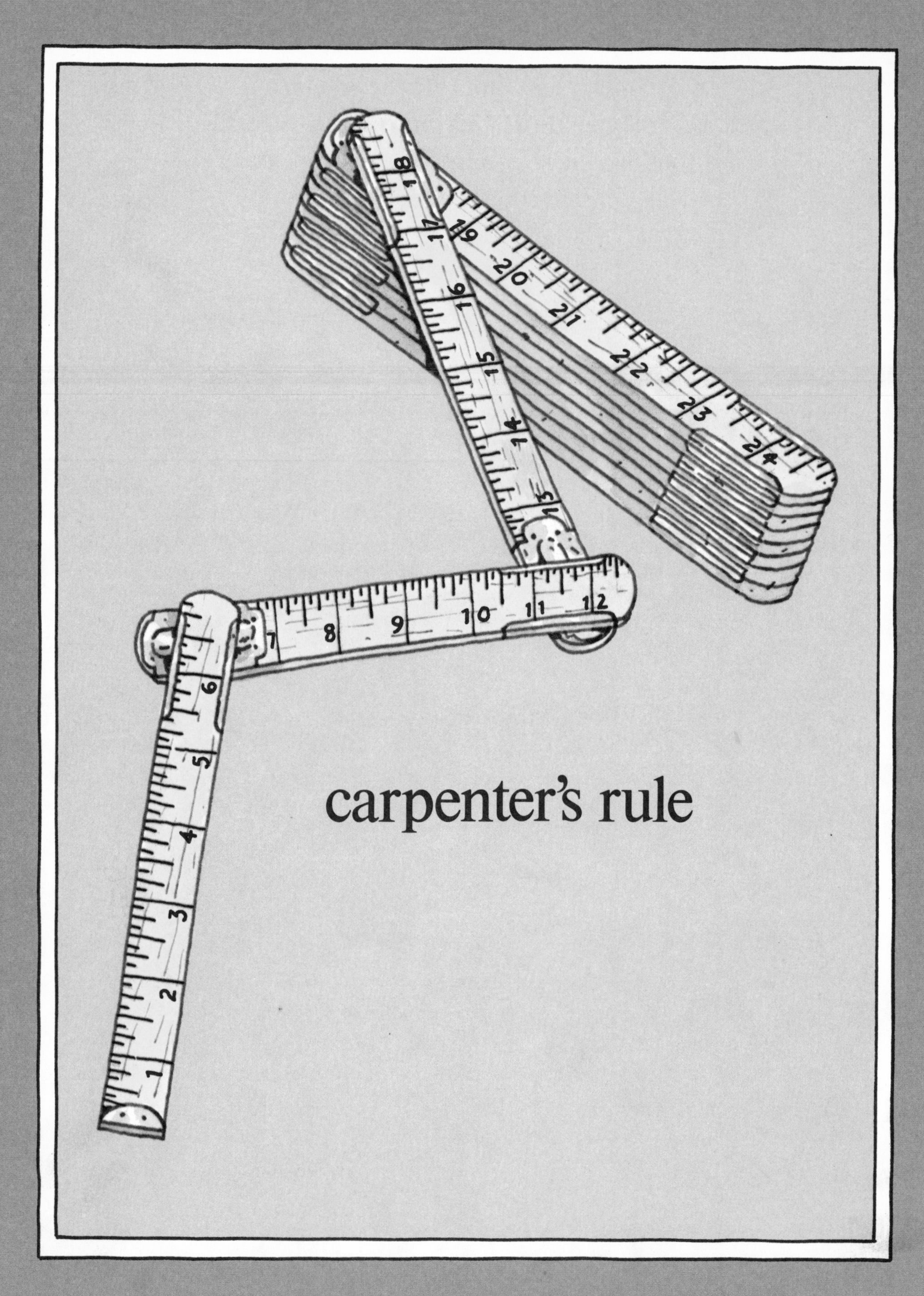
carpenter's rule

The Count uses a carpenter's rule to measure the bat house he is building.

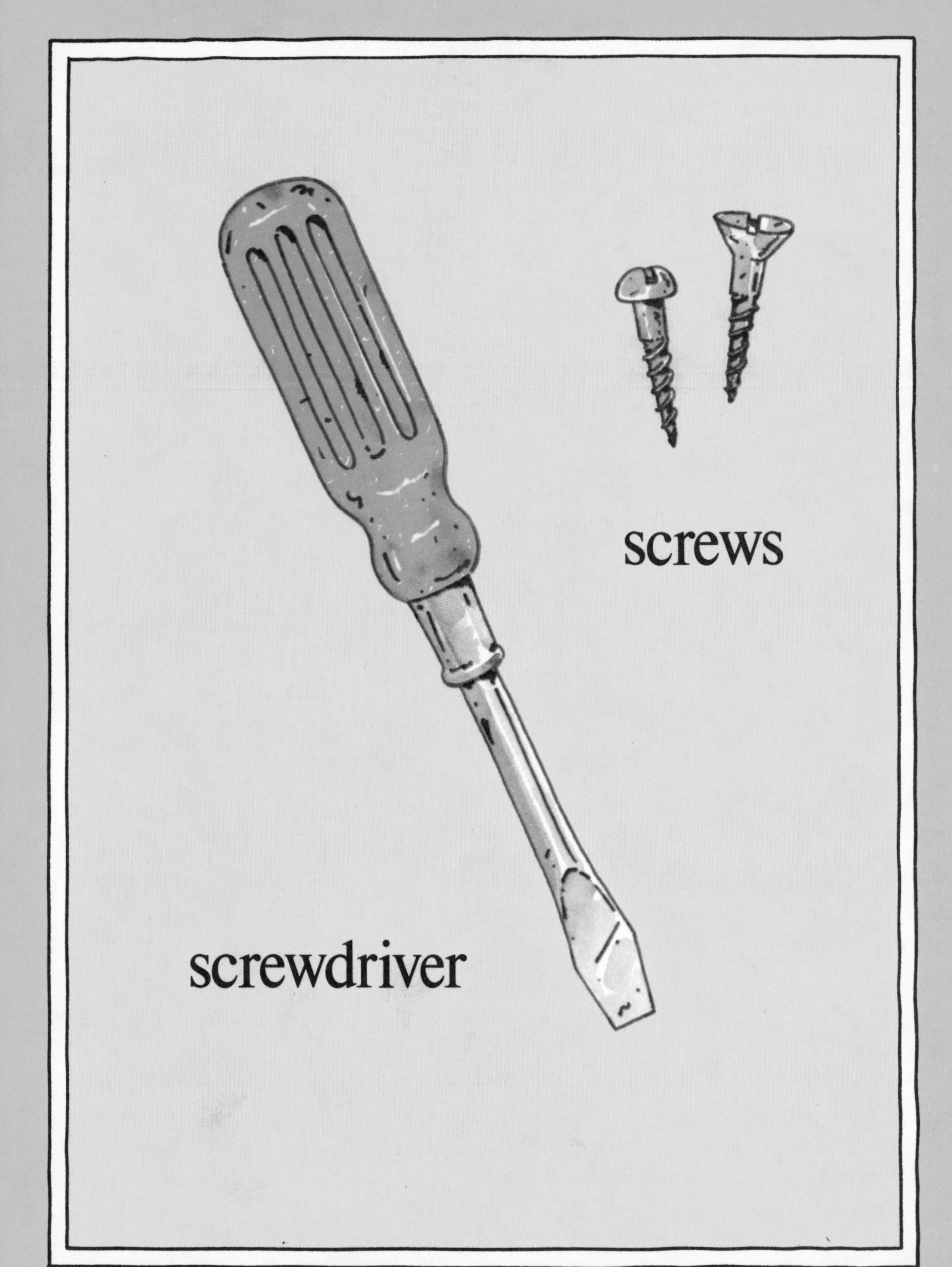
screws
screwdriver

Ernie and Bert are making a new toy chest. Ernie is using a screwdriver to twist in the screws that hold on the hinges.

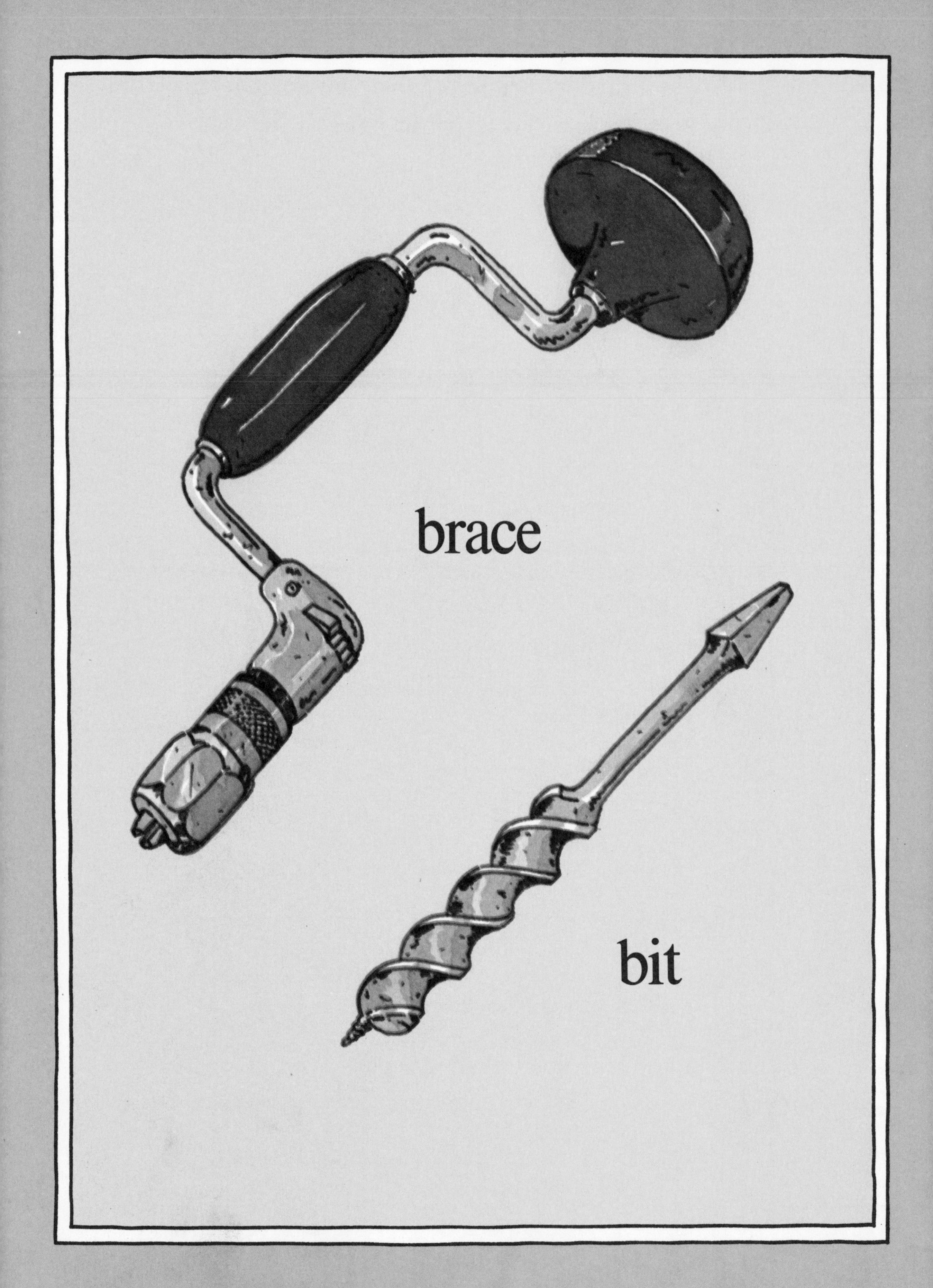
brace
bit

Biff and Sully are drilling holes with a brace and bit. They will put wire through the holes so they can hang up the new sign for Mr. Hooper's store.

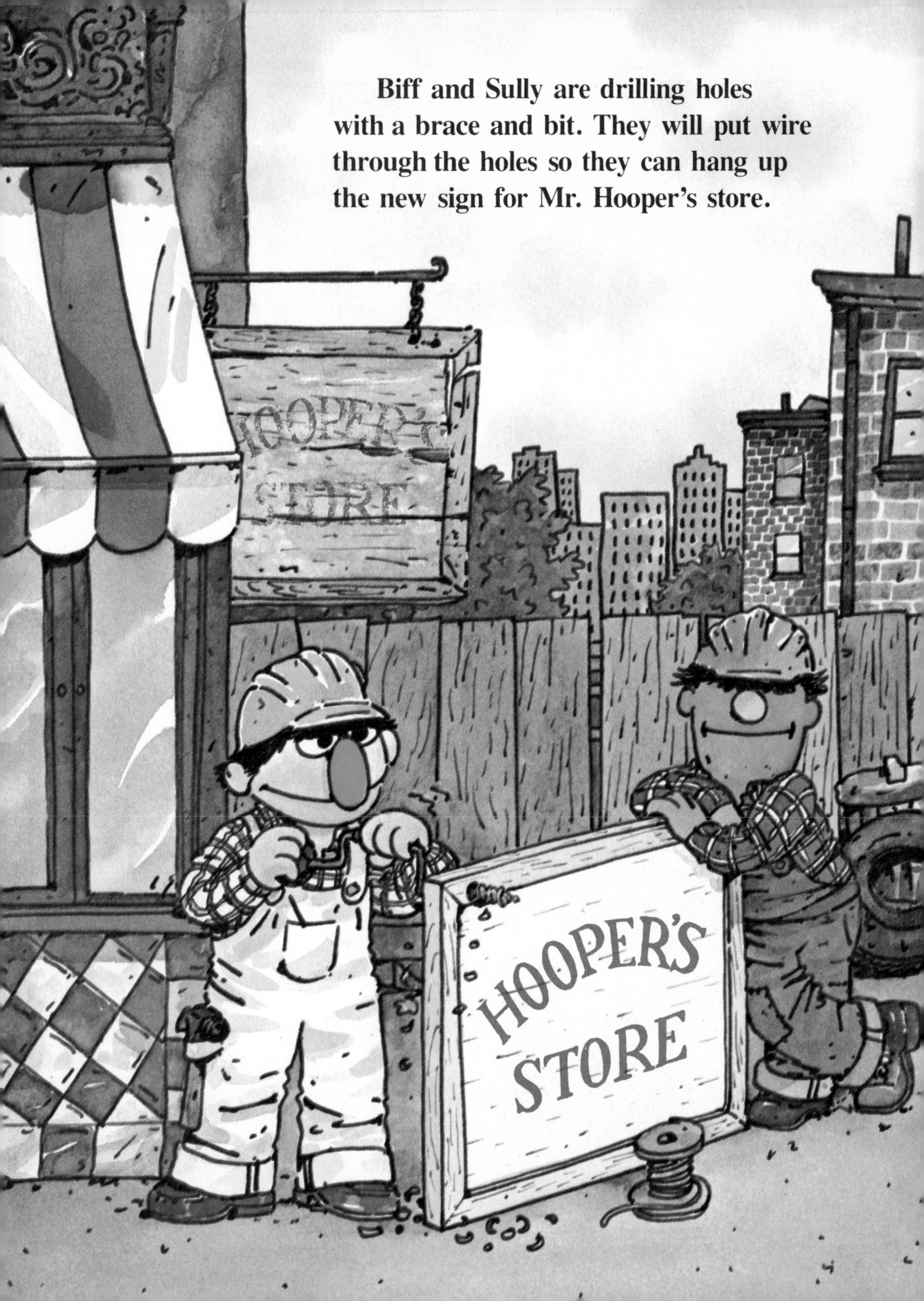

saw

Snuffle-upagus is cutting wood with a saw. He is making a picture frame for his great-uncle's portrait.

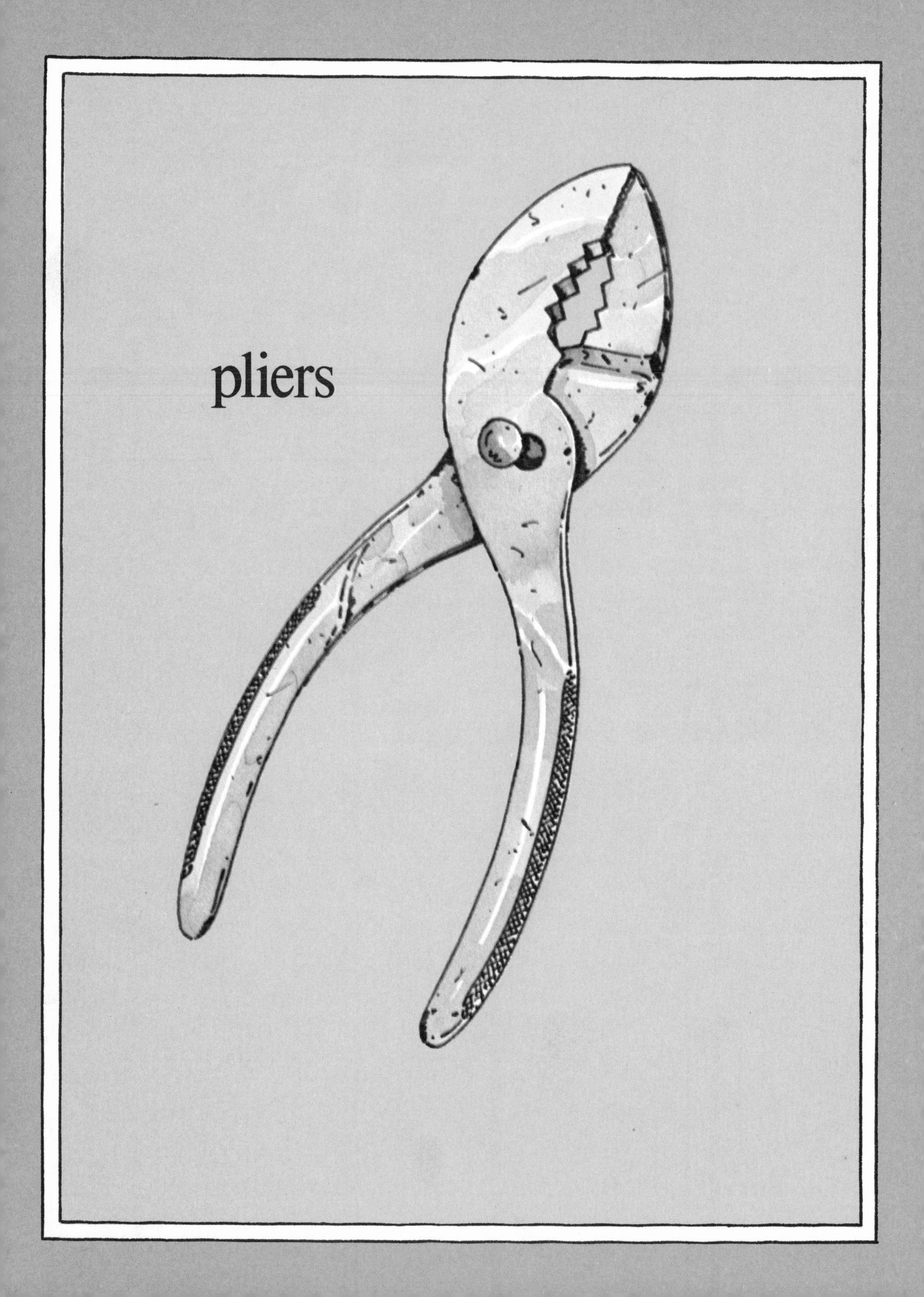
pliers

Farley is putting a name tag on Barkley's collar. He uses a pair of pliers to close the S-hook on the name tag.

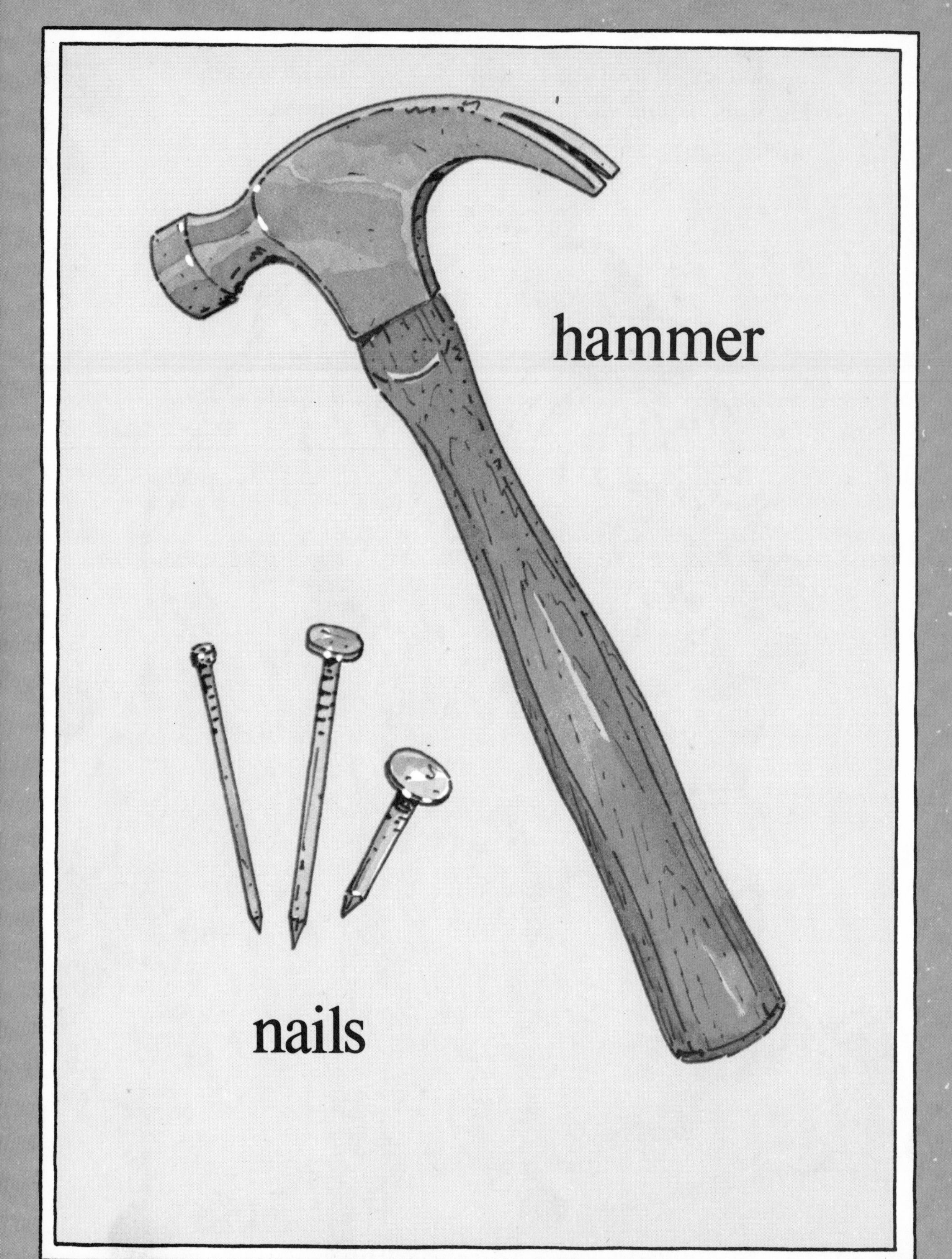
hammer
nails

Herry uses a hammer and some nails to help Big Bird build a new birdseed box.

glue

Prairie Dawn puts glue on all the broken pieces and uses clamps to hold the pieces together.

sandpaper

Grover rubs and rubs with sandpaper to smooth the wood on his mommy's rocking chair.

paintbrush
RAINBOW
PAINTS
paint

After Grover has finished, Betty Lou uses a paintbrush to paint the chair.

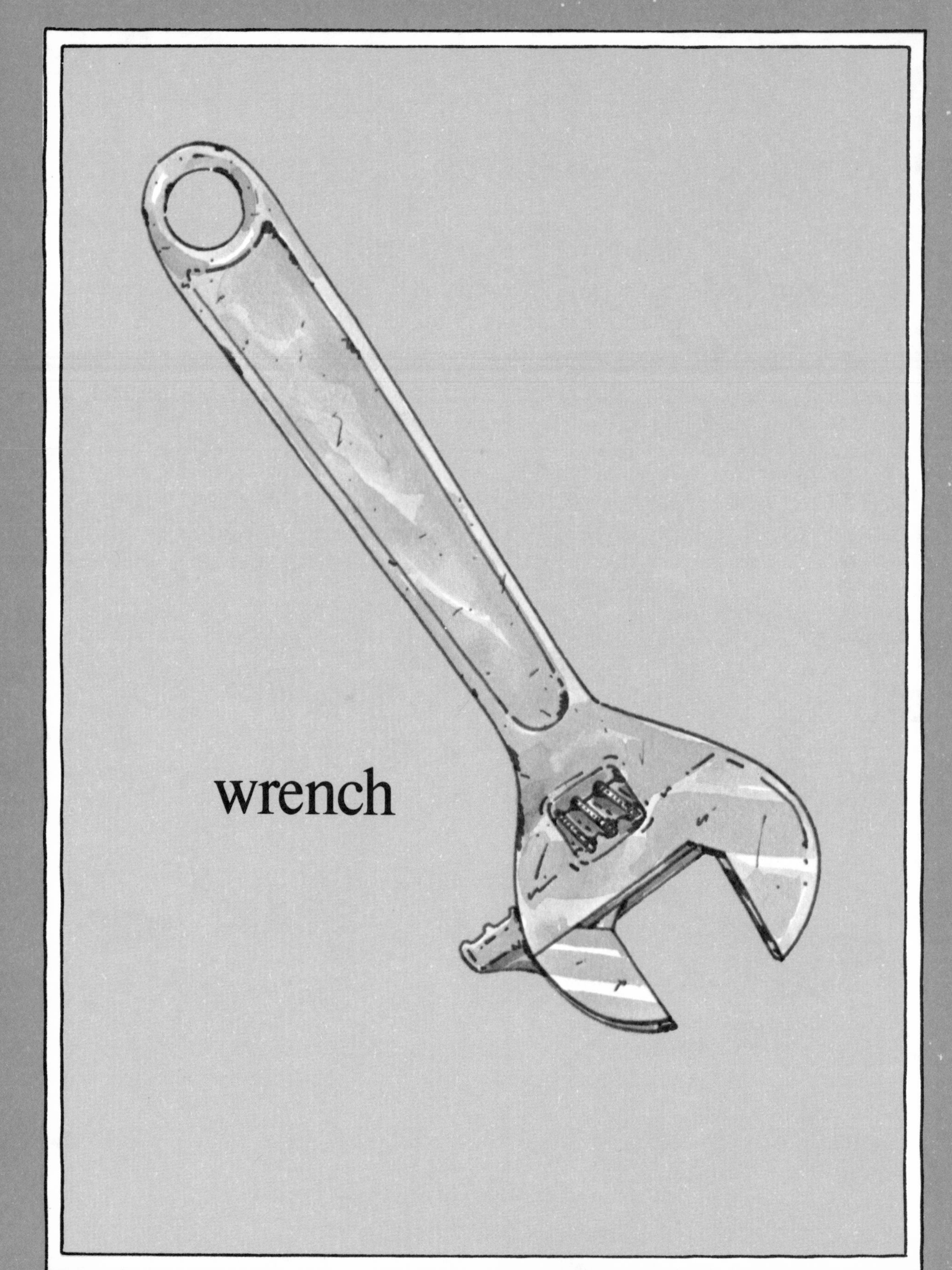
wrench

Do-It Day is almost over and the tools are all put away—except one. David is using the wrench to open the fire hydrant.

Cooling off in the sprinkler is a perfect way to end Do-It Day.